The Soldier in the Cellar

Gettysburg Ghost Gang # 5

By

Shelley Sykes
and
Lois Szymanski

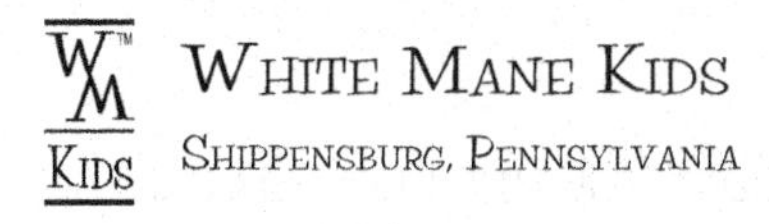

The acid-free paper used in this book meets the guidelines for permanence and durability of the Committee on Production Guidelines for Book Longevity of the Council on Library Resources.

For a complete list of available publications
please write
White Mane Kids
Division of White Mane Publishing Company, Inc.
P.O. Box 708
Shippensburg, PA 17257-0708 USA

Library of Congress Cataloging-in-Publication Data

Sykes, Shelley.
The soldier in the cellar / by Shelley Sykes and Lois Szymanski.
p. cm. -- (Gettysburg ghost gang ; #5)
Summary: When Zach and Philip, along with their friend Chucky, go to Gettysburg, Pennsylvania, to help their aunt with her new house, they find the ghost of a Confederate soldier who also needs their help.
ISBN-13: 978-1-57249-299-8 (alk. paper)
ISBN-10: 1-57249-299-6 (alk. paper)
[1. Ghosts--Fiction. 2. Soldiers--Fiction. 3. Aunts--Fiction. 4. Gettysburg (Pa.)--Fiction.] I. Szymanski, Lois. II. Title.

PZ7.S9834 So 2002
[Fic]--dc21

2002016866

PRINTED IN THE UNITED STATES OF AMERICA

This is for those I would drag into a haunted cellar with me: Amanda and Melissa.

—S.S.

Janice and Guy, who give me a different kind of goose bumps, with all they do.

—L.S.

Contents

Chapter One

The Old House

Philip found his brother, Zach Baxter, and their best friend, Chucky Coppersmith, in the Cavalry Ridge Campground snack bar. He had news to share, but Chucky was deep in concentration, staring down at a typed sheet of paper before him.

"Hmmm..." Chucky held a pencil between his teeth and mused out loud. "I can't remember. Did we have a good turnout for Banana Split Night the last time we had it?"

Philip looked thoughtful. "Was that in May? Yes, it *was* May. I believe we had a fair number of campers in attendance."

Zach giggled and tried to imitate his brother's serious tone. "I believe we had a fair number of campers in attendance." He laughed again. "Do you have to talk like that, Philip? What's up with that anyway?"

"Oh shut up, Zach. Just because you can't put together more than five words in an intelligent sentence..."

"Don't fight," Chucky interrupted them. He was used to their constant spats, but he wanted to finish reviewing his paper. "This is serious. Mom asked me to look at the list of activities she's come up with for next year. She wants to know if there is anything we think could be added, or anything we think was a flop last year. And, she is trying to think of something new that will be fun for the campers coming in at the end of the month from that girls' school." He paused, then added, "Something educational."

Zach looked sheepish. He let out his breath in a puff that blew his bangs upward. "I'm sorry, Chucky."

"Me too. We'll help." Philip plopped down on a stool next to Chucky. He could hear Gloria Coppersmith rattling around in the kitchen behind the snack bar. Chucky's mom worked for Philip and Zach's dad, and lived in a house on the family-owned campground. All of the boys had chores to help in running the campground, but Philip seemed to take it the most serious. "Let me see."

Chucky handed over the paper. He was proud of the great job his mom did as Activities Director

and running the camp snack bar. He wanted all of her events to be a success.

"The jamborees are still on there, aren't they?" Zach asked. The jamborees were his favorite event. Everyone gathered around a bonfire under a starry sky in the main field, roasted marshmallows, made mountain pies and s'mores, and told stories. There were also the funnel cakes, and occasionally a band on the hill. It was a wonderful way to fill an evening!

"Of course jamborees are on the list," Philip said. "It figures you'd like them best. It's all that food!"

"It's not just the food," Zach protested. Then he grinned. "But that part is great!"

Philip smiled too. "Well, there are a bunch on the list."

Zach sighed. "It seems like we never have enough jamborees."

Philip pulled a pencil from his pocket and moved down the list, marking off each activity with a check. "Everything on here looks great," he said, "but I have an idea."

"What's that?" Mrs. Coppersmith had joined them, drying her hands on a red-checkered towel.

"Can we invite a Civil War encampment this year? It would be fun to have a piece of living history here."

Zach rolled his eyes, but he had to agree it was a good idea. He tried to imagine Civil War re-enactors camping on the grounds.

Mrs. Coppersmith was smiling. “That sounds like fun. Maybe we should try it on a small scale at the end of this month. The school administrators would like that. And if it gets a good response we could add it to the schedule for next year.”

Philip grinned and stood up, happy to have had a good idea. “Is Chucky done with his chores?” he asked. “We were hoping he could help us pick the last of the summer tomatoes from our garden.”

Mrs. Coppersmith nodded. “Yes. You boys go on.” She shook her head in disbelief. “It's hard to believe the summer is almost over. The garden produce has been a hit this year, selling well in the camp store.”

Zach snorted. “It oughta be, as hard as we worked.”

“Zach!” Philip steered his brother out of the snack bar. He had to agree they'd worked hard. Not only had they grown and sold a lot of produce, saving for a Swiss camping knife that was still under the glass case in the store, but they'd also found adventure in their garden. Early in the planting, they had dug up a Civil War I.D. tag, and along with it

came the ghost of Corporal Jared Scott, a 5th Michigan Cavalryman who had become a fast friend.

Now, as they walked toward the garden, Philip realized that Mrs. Coppersmith was right. Summer would soon be over. He had mixed emotions about the news he had to share. He and Zach would be leaving the campground for a few weeks. Their dad had asked him to talk to Zach about it, and he figured the garden would be the best place. It was where they always met to talk about anything important.

They pulled two bushel baskets out of the shed and headed toward the middle of the garden, to the rows of tomatoes and green peppers that needed to be picked.

They each knelt in a row of vegetable plants.

"Aunt Penny bought a house in Gettysburg. She's moving to Pennsylvania."

Zach snorted. "I knew that."

"Chucky didn't." He paused. "And Dad wants us to stay with her for a few weeks and help her put her new house in order."

Zach straightened, a large overripe tomato in his hand. "What do you mean?"

Chucky stopped too. "You're going away?"

"For a week or two."

Zach's eyebrows arched. "What are you talking about? This is news to me."

Philip sat down in the dirt between the rows. "You were helping Chucky in the snack bar earlier today when Aunt Penny called. She said the new house is very old, and there is so much to do. She was feeling overwhelmed, so Dad volunteered us to help. He told me to tell you."

"But..."

"Man!" Chucky stood and stuck his hands in his pockets, jiggling the pile of junk inside. "That girls' school is coming to camp. I'm gonna be stuck here with Casey and all those girls! It's not fair!"

"Talk about unfair." Zach blew a big breath of air upwards lifting his bangs. "I was volunteered without ever being asked!"

"Zach, Aunt Penny needs our help and Dad just figured we'd want to help her. After all, she's not just our aunt, she is our godmother!"

No one spoke for a minute, then Zach's face lit up. "Maybe Chucky can go too? It would get him away from all those dumb girls, and it would be more fun for us!"

Chucky and Philip's faces lit up in unison. "Yeah!" Chucky whooped. "I want to go!"

"That *would* be fun," Philip agreed. "Let's ask Dad!"

"And my mom, too," Chucky said with a grin.

* * * * *

Aunt Penny's house was smaller than Philip had expected. A rough, worn, stone cottage, it had been left unattended for years. A variety of weeds and tufts of tall crabgrass mixed in a field that had once been a yard. Ivy vines crawled up the northern side of the house. Leaves lifted flecks of peeling paint from windowsills. They'd been pulling vines away from the house and stuffing them into big plastic garbage bags for the larger part of the morning.

"I'm thirsty," Zach said. "I think I'll see if Aunt Penny has anything to drink." There was just one pile of vines and leaves to finish bagging, so Chucky volunteered. "Go ahead," he said. "You go too, Philip. I'll get this last pile and be right in."

Inside, it was cool and damp, and musty smelling. The boys wrinkled their noses.

"That's just from being closed for so long," Aunt Penny told them cheerfully. She was packing old Mason jars from a kitchen pantry into a box. "I can't believe how much stuff has been left here all these years."

Earlier in the day, Aunt Penny's auburn hair had been pulled up into a pony tail on top of her head, but as the day wore on wisps of curls had fallen from the rubber band, and now there was little left of the pony tail. Her green eyes flashed adventurously. "Who knows what kind of treasure we'll find!"

A chill raced up Philip's spine. Aunt Penny was thinking of treasure, but he had other concerns on his mind. *An old Civil War-era house, built in the mid 1800s, vacant all these years...* He shook away the chills. *There had been too many ghosts already!*

"The realtor said the reason this house was such a bargain was because it was standing unattended for so long," she said. "It *was* a great deal. And if it only means a little extra work, I don't mind!" She put the last jar in a box and spun around looking at her kitchen. "Especially with you boys here to help. It's more like fun than work!" She looked down at the boys. "I love this place. It has so much history and character! Thank you, guys, for all your help."

Zach looked embarrassed, but Philip couldn't help but smile. He was glad to be helping, and he knew what she meant about a little hard work. *Working to make something your own just made you like it better,* he thought. That's how he would feel when they finally bought the Swiss camping knife they'd been saving their garden money for.

"Would you boys mind taking these old jars downstairs and sitting them in the root cellar while I whip up a batch of lemonade? I think we all need a break."

"Sure," Zach said scooping up a box and heading out of the kitchen. He stopped halfway through the door and looked puzzled. "Where is the root cellar?"

"You have to go outside of the house and around back," Aunt Penny told him. "There is an old wooden door to lift. Pull the string at the bottom of the steps to turn on the light."

"Oh, okay." Zach marched out of the kitchen. Philip scooped up a box and followed. They met Chucky at the front door.

"Come on," Philip said. "Follow us. You can lift the door to the root cellar and get the light."

Overgrown bushes overlapped each other and crowded the back yard, making it shady and dark. Philip tightly held the box to his chest as he wedged himself through an opening between the stone wall of the house and a big mountain laurel bush. Chucky followed. He stopped in front of the wooden door. It sat crookedly on a cracked stone foundation. Philip nodded to Chucky and he lifted the creaky door.

It took a moment of feeling around before Chucky found the string and pulled it. A light popped on in the basement and dimly illuminated irregular stone steps.

Philip led them, moving slowly and carefully down the steps. Once he reached the dirt floor at the bottom of the steps he lowered the box and stood straight to look around the cellar. As he raised up he felt a sticky soft trail drape across his face and realized he'd moved into a large spiderweb! Jumping backwards, he almost took out Zach and his box of jars!

"Whoa! Watch what you're doing!" Zach yelped.

"I'm sorry. Spider web," he started to explain, but before he could finish the sentence a sharp screech filled the air. It took a moment for Philip to register the sound. A chill raced up his spine as he realized that the piercing pitch echoing from above was Aunt Penny!

Chapter Two

The Penny

Philip and Zach nearly dropped their boxes of jars as they scrambled toward the door. Philip had to jump over Zach's box, and he followed his brother up the steps and out into the sunlight.

"Aunt Penny!" Zach yelled as he ran through the back door into the kitchen.

When Philip jumped over the wide doorsill and into the kitchen, Aunt Penny was standing by the sink, her hand under running water. "I'm okay, boys. I cut myself."

Chucky joined them. First, he saw Philip and Zach at the sink with their aunt, and then he saw a broken jar in the middle of the floor. "I'll sweep up the glass," he said.

"What happened, Aunt Penny?" Philip asked. He took a paper towel from the roll on the sink and handed it to her.

"Actually, I'm not sure," she said, then turned while wrapping the towel around the fingertips of her left hand. "Thank you, Chucky. I don't know where that came from! I had just wiped out the top shelf of the cabinet when...it sounds crazy, but it was as if that jar just came flying out of there. I didn't see it up there!"

Philip ignored the chill on his neck, and didn't dare glance at Zach. "Maybe you knocked it when you were cleaning," he said.

"I guess I must have," she said. "It startled me, and I screamed. Then I felt so silly that I tried to clean it up too fast."

"Hey, look here," Chucky said. "It's a penny, I think."

They all looked at the penny he held in his hand. It was green with age. Aunt Penny seemed relieved. "That explains it then. I found another jar of pennies when I cleaned the old pantry closet. It was under the bottom shelf, tucked against the wall. I guess someone had started a new penny jar and it must have been up there." She looked at the cabinet above the sink and shrugged.

"You should take a break, Aunt Penny," Philip said. "I thought you were going to be making lemonade."

Aunt Penny ruffled Philip's hair. "I had one more shelf. I'll get to the lemonade now. Did you put the boxes away?"

"We will. Come on, guys," Philip said.

Chucky dribbled the glass from the dustpan to the trash can, put the broom away, and then followed his friends outside again.

They went back to the root cellar. "It's kind of creepy down here," Zach said. The air was cool and smelled damp. Two long shelves ran along the wall opposite the door. A few old tools were scattered on top. A shovel and a pitchfork leaned against the wall. Philip and Zach moved the boxes they had hauled and put them under the shelves.

Chucky cleared his throat. "How did a jar fly off the shelf upstairs?" He pointed up, and they could hear Aunt Penny's footsteps on the creaky wooden floor of the kitchen.

"She hit it," Zach said, and wiped his hands on the back of his jeans.

Philip looked at his brother and pushed the glasses up on the bridge of his nose. "Did she? She said she didn't even see it there."

"Yeah, Zach. And even if she did hit it, she would have had to hit it hard enough to fly out to where it landed." Chucky shoved his hands in his pockets and jingled the junk around in them. "I'd say that's pretty hard."

Zach scratched his head. "I know what you are trying to say. But honestly, we can't find ghosts everywhere we go! It isn't...*normal.*"

"Jars flying? Now that's normal," Philip said.

"Guys, don't," Chucky interrupted them. "And keep your voices down. You want her to hear you? She got scared enough."

Zach sighed. "You're right, Chucky. But really, Philip, I haven't felt any chills or anything like that here. No cold spots. Except for this danged cellar," he said and rubbed his arms.

"Fine, okay," Philip agreed. "But let's keep our eyes and ears open. If there is a ghost here, we can help."

Later that afternoon the boys finished pulling vines and cleaning up the weeds around the foundations. Aunt Penny said she could just picture lots of tulips and daffodils around the sides of the house, and she wanted to plant four o'clocks by the back door. "They smell so sweet in the evening when they open."

Philip could picture it just as she said she wanted it. A small table and chair by the back door where she could read during summer evenings. When she looked up from her book she could look across the backyard to the stone fence that ran along the edge of a farmer's field. Beyond that field, Philip knew, was Gettysburg National Military Park. Lilacs and locust trees sheltered the backyard, and between Aunt Penny and the nearest neighbor stood one of the huge boulders that littered the Gettysburg area.

"If you boys are ready for supper," Aunt Penny said, "I can get the grill started."

"Yes, we're ready," Zach said.

Philip and Chucky agreed. The boys piled the garbage bags in one spot and went to wash their hands. Zach tripped on the wide doorsill.

"I keep forgetting how wide that is," he said.

The walls of the house were over a foot thick, so the doorsills and windowsills were too. The old wooden screen door slapped closed behind them, and they lined up at the sink to wash.

"Can we make two each?" Zach hollered to his aunt.

"Yes," she called back.

They were going to make their own burgers for the grill, and they set to work at the table, which was covered by a new brightly flowered tablecloth. They could hear Aunt Penny humming outside.

"This is fun," Chucky said. "I'm glad I'm not home with Casey. But I do feel bad that no one is going to be around to help her with the stable chores. And I miss Boo!"

"Boo would like it here," Philip said. "Leave some burger for Aunt Penny, Zach!"

Zach pinched a bit of hamburger from the hunk he was forming into a patty and put it back into the package. "I hope Jared tells Boo where we are."

"Yeah. I'm glad we at least got to tell Jared where we were going." Chucky put his two patties onto a paper plate.

Supper was fun. Aunt Penny spread a blanket in the shade of a lilac bush and they had a picnic of burgers, store bought potato salad, fruit salad, and brownies. "I'm afraid you won't get a lot of homemade goodies like you usually do when I see you. But until I get straightened out here, there really isn't time."

Zach wanted to tell her that everything was good, but he was too busy eating.

After supper the boys tackled the main room on the ground floor. It would be Aunt Penny's living room and work room. For now, they pushed boxes up against the walls to make room for the air mattress they were going to be sleeping on that night. They figured that if they slept crossways on it, they would all fit.

"How would you guys like to play some cards before we turn in? Until I get cable installed there isn't much I can get on the TV."

They played cards until sundown, and took turns using the old claw-footed bathtub in the upstairs bathroom. Before they knew it, it was time to go to bed. They said good night to Aunt Penny, who yawned on her way up the steps from the living room.

Chucky lost the coin toss to find out who would be squished in the middle. "Not fair, you guys. I'm heavier, so you guys will roll down on me!" When the laughter stopped and things grew quiet they all felt themselves grow alert.

"This is silly," Zach whispered. "Now I'm wide awake!"

"I know," Philip said. "Me too."

"I am too," Chucky said, and grunted, pushing an elbow at Philip. "But it doesn't look like I'm going anywhere."

* * * * *

Zach moved. Something squeaked. *A mouse?* He moved again. It squeaked again. *The air mattress!* He was thirsty and afraid to wake the others, but Zach decided he'd never get back to sleep if he didn't get up and get a drink of water.

He carefully rolled to his side and swung his legs to the floor. One big *squeak,* and he was standing. Moonlight shone into the kitchen window, and he used that as his guide to the counter and the sink. Not wanting to rummage through the dishes, he cupped his hand under the faucet and drank several handfuls of water. That was better! He wiped his chin with the back of his hand and shook the hand over the basin. Curious to see what the yard looked like at night, he went to the back door and turned the knob. The door creaked as it opened.

"What's going on?" Philip whispered behind him.

Zach jumped and turned. "I was thirsty."

Philip adjusted his glasses on his face. "Then why are you going outside?"

"I'm not. I just wanted to look out there." He sighed. "Oh great. Now Chucky's up too."

Chucky came into the kitchen rubbing his eyes. "What's up?"

"Nothing. Zach's wandering around, that's all."

Zach took a deep breath of night air through the screen door. Beyond the stone wall a mist was moving through the farmer's field. *There must be a stream out there,* he thought. "Hey, do you guys want to go find the stream tomorrow if we have a chance?"

"What stream?" Philip asked standing behind him. Chucky pushed in on his other side. "Whoa, look at that mist," Philip whispered.

"That's gotta be a stream, don't you think?" Zach asked.

As if in answer to his question, a person-sized glob of mist separated from the rest. It almost seemed to crouch, then began to move towards the stone wall.

"What the heck?" Philip bit down on his bottom lip to keep from saying more. But he pushed an arm past Zach, and then pushed the door open, and then pushed Zach out in front of him.

"Philip! I don't want to be out here," Zach said. But he saw the mist move over the wall toward them. It all happened so fast. In one second of time Zach knew he was seeing the ghost of a man who had jumped the wall and was coming toward them. He felt Chucky behind him and saw Philip dash off to follow the mist as it veered off to the left and went around the side of the house.

He was back before Zach could count to 10.

"It went into the root cellar," Philip said as calmly as if he had told Zach and Chucky that the stars were out.

Zach looked back to the field. It was quiet and lit by moonlight.

"Come on, let's go back into the house."

"Philip, I can't go back in there. It's in there," Zach said.

"No, it's in the cellar."

Chucky spoke up. "I think I'm dreaming."

"Come on," Philip said again. "Let's get inside before Aunt Penny wakes up."

Zach didn't want to go, yet he didn't want to stay out there alone either. He wished he'd never been thirsty.

Philip quietly shut the doors. In a small group they moved slowly through the dark kitchen toward the living room and their mattress. Without another word they burrowed into their blankets, all three on their bellies. Philip was so tired he didn't want to think about it until morning.

Just as he thought he could do that, another noise brought them all upright. Something was rolling on the floor. It rolled across the wooden floor right to their mattress. It was Chucky who moved a hand to reach for it.

Philip and Zach moved away from him.

"Oh my gosh," Chucky whispered, then whistled low.

"What is it?" Zach and Philip asked.

"It's the penny. The penny from today, the one that fell with the jar. The same one that I put on the counter. It was on the counter before we went to bed, I know it was!"

Chapter Three

Aunt Penny's Dream

Chucky stared at the penny between his thumb and forefinger. It was the same penny. He could tell by the greenish hue. But how? His fingers shook as he put it on the floor at the head of the mattress and stared at Philip, who rubbed a hand across his brow.

"Man, we can't get away from it, can we?" Zach put his arms under his chin. It's as if when we dug up Jared's I.D. tag we opened the door to another world, and we can't get that door shut again. I almost wish we'd never found that I.D. tag!"

"Zach! You do not wish that!" It was Philip who said it, but Chucky looked shocked too, like he was biting his tongue.

"If we hadn't dug up that tag we'd never have found Jared, and he's an awesome friend." Chucky's eyes were wide.

Zach hung his head. "I just wish he was here."

"Yeah, me too," Chucky said, and Philip nodded in agreement.

All three boys stared off into space. No one moved to pick up the penny. Philip knew it would be a long time before they fell sleep again.

* * * * *

In the morning, the penny was back on the counter. They didn't awaken until Philip heard Aunt Penny calling to them and he shook Zach and Chucky awake. The sun was pouring into the room through the wavy old glass of the living-room windowpane.

"We have so much to do today," Aunt Penny told them. "I thought we could go to town for lunch. I have to pick up some supplies, and you boys deserve a treat!"

"Oh boy!" Zach said. Food!

The boys rose quickly, folded the light blanket they had slept with, and put it on the sofa with their pillows. Then, they leaned the air mattress against the wall and headed into the kitchen for a bowl of cereal.

Midmorning found them on their hands and knees in the kitchen. They'd volunteered to clean the lower cabinets in the kitchen. After Chucky reached inside and pulled out the contents, he handed them to Philip and Zach to put into the boxes that Aunt Penny had given them. There were folded towels that were raggy and covered with dust.

Philip took the top one from Chucky, held it away from himself, and shook out the dust. Then he looked through the stack of folded towels, and opened each one. Creases of dirt made a tic-tac-toe square on each towel. "Look at how different they are," Philip said. "This one is flowered."

"And this one has farm animals on it," Zach said, spreading out another one.

Aunt Penny stooped down to look. "Those are feed-sack towels," she said.

Chucky stopped what he was doing and looked up. "Feed-sack towels?"

"Yes. Years ago, chicken feed and grain for farm animals came in sacks made of colorful material. Families used the material to make dishcloths, curtains, and even feed-sack dresses!"

"Cool!" Chucky loved hearing how different things were in the past.

Aunt Penny took the stack of towels from Philip. "I hope the dirt comes out of these when I launder them," she said. "See what I mean about finding treasures?"

Chucky smiled and stuck his head into the cabinet under the sink. "Phew...more of those canning jars," he said. "I can't believe how many we have already packed off into the root cellar."

"It must have been a lot of work back then," Philip said.

"Whatta ya mean?" Zach was taking the jars from Chucky and placing them in a box beside him.

"Dad said that in the 19th century everything people ate in the winter depended on how hard they'd worked canning in the summer. They jarred the garden vegetables they grew to eat in the winter."

Aunt Penny was scrubbing the walls and listening. "That's right," she added. "They even canned jars of soups and sauces for winter. It was hot, sweaty work. That's why some of the old houses had outbuildings called summer kitchens. That building was used for canning in the summer and kept the whole house from heating up."

Chucky removed the last Mason jar from underneath the sink and handed it to Philip, who slipped it into the box. "After we take these to the root cellar, I'll get a bucket of pine cleaner and water to scrub the inside of the cabinets," he volunteered.

Aunt Penny smiled. "Thank you, Philip," she said. "And then, we will go to town."

"You know, I don't think I even want lunch today," Aunt Penny said. "I am feeling very naughty. I just want to eat a big dessert!"

Zach stared at his aunt, his eyes wide. "Dessert?" He licked his lips.

"And the Lincoln Diner makes the best desserts around. Would you boys like to go there?"

"Sure." Philip and Chucky nodded.

"Can we get a sandwich and a big dessert?" Zach asked.

Aunt Penny ruffled his hair playfully. "You bet!" she said.

* * * * *

The Lincoln Diner sat on the corner of two streets, with the railroad track running right by the diner. Sitting in one of the booths with the etched glass dividers, looking out of the window, Chucky wished for a train to come by. Then he could count the cars and see it up close!

They'd each ordered a hamburger, even Aunt Penny. "We'll still get desserts after we eat," she told them. "We worked hard and we deserve it!"

The boys were watching the activity on the street. There were scores of walkers, most of them summer tourists.

Chucky stared outside, still wishing for the train. He saw a large man striding down the sidewalk. As he got closer, the boys saw the heavy, gray material of the Confederate uniform.

"It's a cavalryman," Chucky hissed, eyes on the sabre that hung from his belt. For a moment he thought it was a ghost.

Aunt Penny looked at Chucky, eyebrows arched. "That's just a Civil War reenactor," she said, her voice full of questions.

"Right," Chucky murmured, his face becoming red.

"We knew that," Philip laughed. "After all, this is Gettysburg."

Aunt Penny looked off into space, staring past the sidewalk people. "It's strange that we should see a Confederate soldier today, though," she said. "After..."

"After what?" Philip leaned forward, his elbows on the table.

"It's nothing, really," Aunt Penny said. "It's a dream I had last night."

"About a Confederate soldier?" Chucky was excited.

"Yes." Aunt Penny's voice sounded soft. "I dreamed he was in the house. He came into my bedroom and stood there."

"Then what?" Now Zach was excited.

"He looked so sad. He stared at me for a moment, then he said, 'You have to read my letter.' I just sat there, my mouth hanging open as he faded away. 'Please read my letter,' he said, and then he disappeared, just faded away into thin air."

Aunt Penny smiled, rejoining them from some faraway place in her mind. "It was just a dream. But it all came back to me, seeing that soldier there. Last night, it seemed so real."

Chucky stared across the booth at Philip and Zach on the other side. He was sure they were all thinking of the soldier they'd seen the night before. The soldier made of mist. The soldier that disappeared into the root cellar.

Just then there was a rumbling, and the diner started to shake a little.

"The train!" Chucky watched it approach. Then, it was beside them, rumbling down the track and past the diner.

Aunt Penny grinned. "Stare hard at the train and you will feel like it is standing still and we are the ones moving!"

Chucky stared into the windows of the train as it rushed past. A smile spread across his face. "It does feel like we're moving!"

"Yes, it does." Both Philip and Zach were smiling.

Chucky watched the train, feeling like he was aboard, and he thought about the Confederate soldier. He let his mind go blank, feeling himself move with the train. Then his mind moved in a different direction. He saw a jumble of gray, and mist, and a soldier, and he sighed. What were they going to do?

Chapter Four

Scaredy-Cat

Chucky concentrated on the rag in his hand as he washed the window near the back door. After several drops of water hit him on the head he stepped back and looked up. Zach's arm reached out of the window just above Chucky, and it held a long squeegee.

"Hey, Zach, be careful up there."

Zach's arm disappeared and his head popped out of the window a second later. "Sorry, Chucky, but it's hard to wash these old windows from the inside." He moved forward a little further and looked down at the ground. "Yikes. Maybe we should ask if we can wash them from outside with a hose."

"That might be better," Chucky said. "I'm going to have to stand on a chair to get the top of this window."

"Chucky, look," Zach said, as he pointed towards the stone wall and the field beyond.

Chucky turned, but didn't see anything. The first thing that came to his mind was the mist, the ghost that had leaped over the wall. But it was daytime and the sun shone brightly, and there was no mist. "What is it?"

"It's a big, fat cat."

"It's probably looking for a mouse in the corn stubble."

"Chucky, go and see if you can get near it."

"I'm not going back there. We're supposed to be cleaning windows."

A voice at his elbow made Chucky jump.

"Aren't you working?" Philip asked. He'd come around the side of the house with an empty bucket. "I need more water. How about you?"

"No, I'm fine. Zach says there's a cat back there over the wall."

Philip looked up to where Zach had been hanging from the window, but saw no sign of him. A few moments later Zach came out of the back door.

"Come on. We can take a break."

Chucky and Philip followed Zach who broke into a trot and headed to the wall at the far end of the yard. He had clambered over it and landed on the other side when they reached it. As he climbed the low 3-foot wall, Chucky could see the back of the tabby cat. It was facing away from them, in a crouched, hunting position.

Zach was more careful now. He took a few slow steps toward the cat and squatted, holding one hand outward. "Here, kitty. Here, kitty, kitty."

The cat's ears twitched, but it didn't move otherwise. Chucky and Philip knelt, one on either side of Zach. "Here, kitty," Philip tried.

In a quick jerky movement the cat turned its head to look at them, then looked away. It flicked its tail in an aggravated wave.

"We're messing up its hunting," Chucky said.

"I don't know," Philip said. "Did you see its tail? It's all puffy like he's afraid."

Chucky nodded. "It's just mad at us."

"Listen," Zach whispered.

They strained their ears. A low grumbling came from the big tabby.

"That cat sees something," Chucky said.

"I want to see him," Zach said and stood up. He had taken just one more step toward the cat when it began to rise. Zach stopped. The cat stood and seemed as if it grew taller. Its back was arched high, and its tail was puffed out. It cried a strange, long yowling sound.

Chucky and Philip stood up, too. Philip tried to see what the cat was reacting to. But there was nothing! In the warm late afternoon sunshine he felt a coolness settle around him.

Then, the cat's head began to move. It seemed as if it was watching something in the air that moved slowly from their left to their right. Chucky thought about the column of mist they had watched the night before, and how it had broken off and moved across the wall. Did the cat see something like that?

Finally, whatever had passed in front of the cat was gone. The cat cried and jumped away, running off to their left in a blur of dark gray.

The boys looked at each other. Philip noticed the warmth coming back. "I didn't see anything, but I know what that was."

"I wish Corporal Scott could be here with us," Chucky said.

"So do I," Zach agreed. "Philip, isn't there a way we can get him here? He'd know what to do."

Philip pushed his glasses up on the bridge of his nose. "Sure he would. And we'll have to find a chance to talk to him."

"Maybe Aunt Penny will take us home for a visit," Zach said. "You have to figure out a way we can do that without everybody getting suspicious."

"Why would anyone get suspicious?" Philip asked. "It's not like we live a long way from here. We'll talk to Aunt Penny tonight."

"Yeah, tonight," Chucky said. "Your aunt rented that video for us to watch, remember? As if we need a video to see what a ghost looks like."

Philip laughed quietly. Aunt Penny had rented a copy of a new ghost movie for them to watch. "We can't exactly tell her that, can we?"

* * * * *

That night the boys lay on their air mattress, propped up on their elbows and eating from the big bowl of popcorn in front of them. Aunt Penny curled up in her armchair, one foot dangling over the edge.

"I thought this wasn't supposed to be this scary," she said, eating a mouthful of popcorn. "Are you boys going to be able to sleep tonight?"

They looked at her and nodded. Philip wanted to tell her about some of the stuff they had experienced: an RV that rocked them off their feet, being surrounded by a circle of ghostly soldiers. But instead he said, "We'll be okay. But what about you, Aunt Penny? Do you believe in ghosts?"

Chucky and Zach looked at her, too, eager to hear her answer.

"I'm interested in them. But I never thought about it much. So, you boys believe in ghosts?"

"Oh, yes, ma'am," Chucky answered. "Mr. Nesbitt does, too, and he's a friend of ours."

"That author."

Philip nodded. "He comes to the campground to sign books."

Aunt Penny nodded and turned back to the movie. The boys looked at each other and shrugged. Philip thought, *It would be so much easier if she believed in ghosts.*

After the movie ended they helped Aunt Penny clean up. Philip dried a wet glass that she had handed him. All of them got ready for bed.

"Thanks for today, Aunt Penny, for the movie and the ice cream, everything."

"You're welcome. You have been a big help to me. I'd have been so lonely here with all this work to do myself."

"Won't you be lonely after the work is done and you're here all the time?"

"I don't think so. Then it will be a place to live, a real home. And I can invite you over all the time, and come visit you as well. It's so wonderful to be living this close to your father and you boys."

"That's what Dad said about you." Philip put the glass away and took the one she held. "I was wondering if we can go see Dad. Just a visit. We can get fresh clothes so we don't have to go to the laundromat. And—"

"I don't see why not. Maybe I'll call him. We can do dinner together tomorrow. Would you like that?"

Philip nodded and grinned. They'd have to spend most of the time with Dad, but surely he'd be working and they could find a minute or two to go talk to Jared. As he thought about that he could hear Chucky and Zach talking in the living room.

"You just don't want to sleep in the middle again, Chucky. Quit stalling and get in bed."

"Philip's not in bed yet. I don't have to get in bed yet." He was at the side of the room going through the junk he had in his pockets. He pulled the green penny from the pile. "I'm keeping this," he said.

Zach looked at what Chucky held in his fingers. "I wouldn't keep that."

"If it's in my pocket with all that other stuff, it might not roll around all night."

"Or else, all the stuff in your pockets will be dumped out in the morning."

"I hadn't thought of that," Chucky said.

"Just put it all back and get in bed!"

"Oh, all right, Zach."

When Philip finally joined them, Chucky was squeezed into the middle again. Aunt Penny said good night and turned off the overhead light. She left the light on above the stove, as a night light. No one spoke until Aunt Penny's footsteps finally stopped.

"We're going home tomorrow for a visit," Philip whispered. "We'll have to make time to find Jared while Dad is working. It shouldn't be too hard."

"That's perfect," Zach said.

"My shoulders hurt," Chucky said, and yawned.

"Mine do too," Zach and Philip said at the same time. "I'm tired," Philip added.

"Let's get some real sleep tonight," Zach said.

Chucky mumbled something into the mattress. It sounded like: "Nothing's going to wake me up."

The next morning proved Chucky right. Nothing had woken him. All three boys had been so bone tired they'd slept all night long. But when Philip went to the kitchen and saw the sleepy look on his aunt's face he knew she hadn't been as lucky.

Aunt Penny was sipping coffee at the table. Her hair wasn't brushed and there were circles under her eyes.

"What's wrong, Aunt Penny?"

She jumped. "Oh, Philip, good morning."

"You look like you've been up all night."

"It was a cat. It woke me around four o'clock and I couldn't get back to sleep."

"What cat?"

"I don't know. It was crying in the back yard. I heard it when I woke up from the dream."

"You dreamed about the soldier again?" Philip sat beside her.

"Silly, isn't it? I shouldn't bother you with my dreams. It was probably caused by the scary movie before bedtime."

"Was it the soldier?"

"Yes. It was him again. Only this time, he called me by name. 'Penny. Penny.' He repeated it over and over."

Chapter Five

Gushing Girls, a Poodle, and a Mission

Chucky stared at Philip. "She said it kept saying, 'Penny, Penny, Penny'?"

"That's right. That's what she said," Philip agreed. He took his pajama top from the air mattress, folded it, and placed it on top of the bottoms he'd just folded.

Zach flopped down on the big overstuffed chair. "Isn't it odd how she keeps dreaming about that soldier?"

"Not so strange," Philip said. He lowered himself onto the air mattress, then rolled over on his back to stare at the ceiling. "Think about it. We know she has a ghost soldier staying in the root cellar. He must be trying to tell her something."

"That's what I think." Chucky spoke louder than he had intended to, and both boys looked up. He rooted in his pocket, removed the old penny, and held it up for them to see.

"The penny. So?" Zach blew his bangs upward and sniffed.

"Don't you see? The penny keeps trying to get our attention. Or maybe it's not the penny. Maybe it is the ghost's way of telling us he has a message for Aunt Penny."

Philip thought you could probably hear a penny drop, they were all so quiet. It made him think. The penny coming to them. The dreams Aunt Penny kept having. The soldier in the cellar. Philip shrugged. Pennies, Mason jars, and Confederate soldiers. It just didn't add up, unless Chucky was on to something.

"And how about that cat?" Zach asked. "He saw something for sure. Do you think it was the root cellar ghost, or something else?"

Philip shrugged. "I don't know, but tonight, when we go home for the cookout, I think we should talk to Jared. He'll know what to do."

Zach grunted. "We need more than advice. We need Jared to come back with us and check things out. I don't know if I can handle one more ghost."

Zach looked so serious that Chucky couldn't help but grin at him.

Philip looked at Zach and smiled, too. "Hmmm. Jared coming here. Now that's a thought."

* * * * *

When Aunt Penny turned into the camp lane, the first thing the boys noticed was how the whole area was teaming with girls. "Oh my," Chucky groaned. "We've been invaded!"

Zach snickered. "It's that girls' school." He looked around and grinned. "This may be worse than ghosts!"

Philip answered with an air of superiority. "If we stay out of their way, they will stay out of ours."

Zach rolled his eyes and watched Philip open the car door and partially step out. He was immediately surrounded by girls.

"This is Philip," Casey gushed. "Didn't I tell you he was cute?"

Philip's ears turned red. He leaned back into the car.

"Philip can help you with anything around the campground," she continued. "He knows it all. So girls, whichever one of you needs a special friend..." Her voice trailed off and Zach grinned at the embarrassment he saw on his brother's face. But a moment later the grin was replaced with a blush of his own.

"Just remember, girls, Zach is mine." Casey leaned into the car window on Zach's side and two girls crowded on either side of her. "Isn't he adorable?"

Chucky coughed and Casey leaned further into the window. "Oh yuck. That's my brother Chucky in the middle."

Now Chucky blushed.

"Girls, girls, girls!" Aunt Penny scolded. "Let the boys out of the car." She tried to hide the smile on her face. She turned to the boys and put on a fake accent. "You boys are stars," she said. "Do you have any comments for the press?"

Each of the boys groaned. They climbed out of the car. Six or seven girls, ages nine to twelve, stared, smiled, and batted their eyes.

"Oh gross," Chucky moaned. "Carbon copies of Casey. One is enough!"

They headed to the house, but before they reached the front door, Casey skipped in front of Chucky. "Just wait until you see what I got," she said. "Yesterday, Mom bought a present for me in town. Remember, she said she'd think about it?"

Chucky's heart sank. *A dog*, he thought. *She got the dog I always wanted.* He could picture the hound of his dreams, with long droopy ears and sad eyes. "A dog?"

"Yep!" Casey's smile spread across her face like marmalade on warm toast. "She is so pretty. Come on, you gotta meet Prissy!"

Zach grinned. "Yes, let's go meet Prissy!"

Chucky followed Casey into the house. Zach and Philip followed them. As soon as Casey opened the kitchen door the boys started to laugh. Even Chucky chuckled, as he looked at the little white poodle with pink bows on its ears that danced around on its hind legs, begging for attention.

Chucky shook his head. *Not the dog of my dreams*, he thought. *Definitely not the dog of my dreams!*

* * * * *

Philip let his eyes wander over the garden. They had been gone less than a week, but it felt much longer. Overripe tomatoes hung from vines on large green plants that sprawled on their sides, heavy with fruit. Suddenly it hit him, they had done it all on their own. The beautiful garden plot that had made all the money they'd been saving in the tin box under the registration counter was theirs and theirs only. It felt good. He glanced at Zach and Chucky, sprawled on their sides on the grassy edge of the garden and he wondered if they were thinking the same thing. Stepping through the crowded rows he made his way across the garden to hear what they were talking about.

The air smelled like burning charcoal and steaks grilling. Soon, Dad would call them to eat.

"Too many girls for me," Chucky drawled softly. His hand moved up and down in a strange motion. As he drew closer, Philip saw why. Boo had found Chucky, and was getting a thorough scratching behind the ears. "I'd be happy if it was just me and old Boo here."

Zach snickered. "Aren't you feeling a little jealous of Casey? Are you sure you don't want to invite little Prissy to meet ol' Boo?"

Chucky covered Boo's ears and faked a horrified look. "No poodle's going to make my sensible hound take leave of his senses."

Philip settled cross-legged in the grass beside them. "For a minute there, you sounded like Jared," he said.

Zach looked around. "Where *is* Jared? I thought he would have found us by now."

"Probably being ambushed by girls," Chucky said dryly.

"Aw, they aren't that bad."

Chucky looked at Zach as though his friend had lost his mind. "Yes, they are."

"Look how long it took us to shake them just so we could be alone," Philip added.

"He's right," Chucky agreed. "God help us if they discover our garden. They'll want to weed, and water, and win us over."

"Who will want to win you over?"

The boys jumped when they heard the voice they were so fond of.

"Jared." Philip said with a nod.

"We missed you," Zach added.

"Did you miss us?" Chucky asked.

"We need help," Zach snorted. "We need your help bad."

"Whoa, boys. It hasn't even been a week. Now what have you gotten yourselves into?"

A sudden silence fell upon the garden plot as each boy looked at one another. Pausing, Chucky nudged Philip's knee. "You tell him," he said, and Philip leaned forward. *What should he tell first?*

The smell of campfires cooking steaks and corn, and the sound of laughter drifted on the breeze as Philip took a deep breath. *I sure hope he can help,* he thought. He looked into Jared's eyes and began to tell him about the cat, the penny, the column of mist, the root cellar ghost, and the soldier in Aunt Penny's dreams.

Chapter Six

Jared's Harrowing Ride

Zach got a bad attack of the giggles on the way back to Aunt Penny's house. He sat in the back seat next to Chucky and tried to stifle it with his hand. Chucky tried to keep his eyes on the back of Philip's head, but it was hard not to look toward the roof of the car. He knew what Zach was laughing about and he was afraid he'd start laughing too. He wondered how Philip could stand being so still in the front seat next to his aunt.

"I'm so full," Aunt Penny said as they rode on the dark road. "And tired. I think I'll get to bed early tonight," she said, yawning. "What about you boys?"

Philip nodded. He was about to answer her when suddenly the car braked and he felt himself sliding forward in the seat until he was stopped by his seatbelt.

"Hold on!" Aunt Penny yelled.

Even Zach stopped giggling in time to look and see the deer that had jumped in front of Aunt Penny's car. She'd stopped just in time to keep from hitting it. Two more deer followed the first, with graceful leaps across the road.

"Is everybody alright?"

The boys nodded and agreed. "There are so many deer around here," Philip said.

"I'll have to remember that. Phew! I think I'm wide awake again," his aunt told them with a nervous laugh. Soon the car was moving steadily along.

Chucky couldn't help looking up at the roof of the car. And in a moment, he was giggling too. Zach heard him and started laughing.

"What is so funny, you two?" Aunt Penny asked. She sounded cheerful, all of the nervousness gone from her voice.

Philip turned in the seat to look at them. Chucky was glad it was pretty dark. He pointed up. Instead of laughing, Philip made a stern face at them. "They are just being goofy, Aunt Penny."

She drove the car into the weed-rimmed driveway. Chucky and Zach unbuckled their seat belts and jumped from either side of the car. Jared, the reason for their giggles, let go of the luggage rack and slid to the ground.

Philip gave him a nod. "Aunt Penny, can we go to see if that cat is in the field?"

"Yes, but don't be long. I think I'll make a cup of tea."

Corporal Scott was fidgeting with his uniform while she went inside out of earshot. He pulled at his cuffs, yanked at the hem, and tugged at the collar. He followed the boys a little way from the door.

"How did you like the ride?" Zach asked, bursting into laughter again.

The fidgeting ghost stopped what he was doing and tilted his head to the side. "I must say, that's the fastest I've ever moved. Almost kept right on going when the deer crossed in front of us though."

Philip laughed for the first time. "I half-expected to see you slide down the windshield and tumble onto the road. You're a good rider!"

"And that's a mighty fast horse," the corporal said. "Now, if you'd like to show me around, let me get my bearings, I'll see what I can do."

"Okay," Philip said. "Let's start with the field."

They walked to the stone wall and showed Jared where they had seen the misty column and told him how the one foggy shape had slipped out of the column and had come over the wall.

"It moved down here and came around the side of the house. It went into the root cellar. We'll show you." Philip put a finger to his lips as they crossed the side of the house. With slow, deliberate movements, he lifted the root cellar door and laid it gently back and open. "Down here," he whispered.

"We should have a flashlight," Chucky whispered. "But at least I remembered to bring the gun."

Philip and Zach nodded, but Jared recoiled and blinked. "The gun? What gun?"

Chucky reached around behind him and pulled something from his back pocket. "Not a gun for shooting. This one."

He held the gunlike object out in front of him and pushed a button. A small display window glowed a greenish yellow. Numbers flashed. "It displays temperature readings."

"You got it from the ghost hunter," Jared said.

"Yes. He gave it to us," Zach whispered.

Philip knew that Jared Scott did not like to talk about Byron Skelly, the ghost hunter who had come in search of ghosts and caused a stir in the ghost community of the Cavalry Ridge Campground. "He gave us the other gadget, too. But we don't use it."

"We'd never use the zapper," Zach added.

"Let's get down there," Chucky hissed. "We don't have much time."

He felt his way down the stairs in the dark, taking each step slowly. At the bottom of the steps, he reached for the light string, then pulled it. There was a snapping sound and a brief flash of light. "Darn," Chucky said. "I think the bulb just burned out."

"It's okay," Philip said. "We have Jared's glow."

The display in front of Chucky jumped a little, the temperature decreasing by degrees as he entered the cooler, dirt cellar. "You guys stay a little behind me while I take readings."

Chucky thought it was easier for him to be in the dark cellar if he had the job of reading the temperature. He could keep his eyes on the display and not worry about the creepy living beings that might be there with him. He wasn't exactly afraid of spiders and mice, but he didn't like having the unfair advantage of being seen first.

"The average temperature seems to be...52 degrees." Chucky turned his whole body easily to the left and then slowly around. "Yeah, it seems to be...whoa!"

"What is it?" Zach asked, pressed against Chucky's back.

"This corner!" Chucky said. "It's showing 33 degrees! That's almost a 20-degree drop."

Philip was behind him now. "We can subtract, Chucky."

"That means there is something here!" Chucky was excited and didn't take Philip's comment the wrong way. "Do you see anything, Corporal Scott?"

Jared moved around them and came to stand in front of Chucky. The temperature fluctuated again, the numbers flashed and settled slightly colder. "Turn off that gadget, son," Jared said.

Chucky reluctantly did as he was asked and was relieved to see he wasn't left in the dark. Their ghost friend's soft blue glow touched the walls of the cellar.

Jared moved a step toward the corner and crouched down. "Hello," he said. "Can you hear me?"

Zach gripped the back of Chucky's shirt. Philip pressed in close to them. At times like this it seemed as if the boys pressed into the tightest little knot they could manage.

"I know you are here," Jared was saying. "I am just like you. I can feel you here. Let me talk to you."

Philip wondered why Jared was not seeing the ghost. He'd never had trouble before as far as he knew. *Why can't a ghost see a ghost? Could they hide from each other?*

"We want to know what is wrong. I'm Jared Scott. Why don't you tell me your name? I think your name is Harmon. Is it Harmon?"

"What's happening?" Chucky whispered.

Jared flung his hand backward, telling him to be quiet. Chucky thought that he could bear it no longer.

"Boys! Are you down there?"

Chucky bit his tongue when all of them jumped suddenly.

"Right here, Aunt Penny, coming," Philip said.

"I'll catch up with you," Jared said. The boys went quickly up the steps into the night air. Chucky turned off the temperature gun and shoved it back into his pocket.

"What are you doing in the dark cellar?"

Philip reached for the door and closed it in place, shutting out the blue glow that Aunt Penny couldn't see. "I heard something. I thought a cat was down there. But when we opened the door, nothing came out, so we went down there to make sure it wasn't in the cellar."

"In the dark?"

"The light bulb burned out when we pulled the string."

"Well, the water is heating for tea. And I don't like you in the cellar at night. There could be rats living down there."

"Sorry," they said, wondering if rats were really her concern.

It wasn't easy to sit at the bright kitchen table drinking tea while wondering what was happening in the creepy cellar. Philip wondered what his aunt would think if she knew there were two ghosts not that far beneath her feet. Chucky tried to keep from looking at the floor, just as he'd had trouble not looking at the roof of the car. Zach felt the same way, but there were no giggles this time.

There was no way they could sleep until they'd seen Jared, and long after Aunt Penny had gone to bed the boys were sitting up on the air mattress waiting for a sign. When the blue glow finally came into their room from the kitchen, Philip whispered, "In here."

Jared came to them with a sad look on his face. He was a soldier who didn't have to tell anyone that his mission had failed.

"You didn't have any luck," Philip said.

"No, I didn't."

"There is a ghost there," Chucky said.

"Oh, I know that, son. He's there. But he guarded himself from me, blocked me out in a way I'm not familiar with. But I do know two things. He is very sad and in need of help. And he's afraid of me."

"Afraid of you?" Zach asked.

"He's a Confederate, Zach. I'm what he's running from. I don't know if I can ever get him to talk to me."

The boys didn't answer. They knew that if Jared couldn't help him there would be a slim chance of ridding the ghost of whatever held him there.

Chapter Seven

Enlisting a Confederate

Chucky couldn't stop thinking about the ghost. He thought about it long into the night, while Zach and Philip slept on either side of him on the big air mattress. He thought about it while he was weeding the flower bed that edged the back wall of the house, especially when he worked his way around the root cellar door. And he thought about it while sitting at the kitchen table with Zach and Philip waiting for Aunt Penny to finish making grilled cheese sandwiches for lunch.

He must feel so alone, he thought. *He has no friends, no one to talk to. And he's too afraid to talk to the corporal.* He shook his head, feeling sad.

"What are you shaking your head for?"

When Chucky looked up he saw Zach staring at him curiously. He saw that Philip was watching him, too. He didn't realize he had moved at all.

"I was just thinking about..." He paused, wondering what Aunt Penny would think if he said, *I was just thinking about the ghost down there*. Aunt Penny faced the stove, watching the cheese sandwiches sizzle. Chucky pointed at the floor and started over. "I was just thinking about," his finger jabbed the air, and he hesitated, pointing down, "all kinds of stuff."

Zach looked at the floor, then at Chucky.

"I guess I was thinking about how some folks aren't lucky enough to have friends, or anyone to talk too, and how lonely that must be. And I was thinking about how lucky we are to have each other."

Aunt Penny turned around and smiled. "You have such a kind heart, Chucky."

Chucky squirmed, embarrassed.

Aunt Penny didn't notice. She flipped a sandwich with the metal spatula and continued to talk. "I don't know why, but lately I've been thinking about those kind of things too, especially about how folks felt during the wartime. Ever since I moved into the house I've been thinking about how friends and families fought against each other in the Civil War, and how hard it must have been for those men." She stopped, sliding a grilled cheese out of the pan and onto a plate. "And I keep having these dreams."

All of the boys were still, listening to Aunt Penny. Philip felt as if he couldn't breathe. *Why was Aunt Penny having those thoughts? Was the ghost affecting her, too?*

"What kind of dreams?" Zach asked.

"About a soldier. At first it wasn't clear. But now I can see him in my dream. He's so young, practically a boy, and he has streaks of dirt on his face, and he wants me to help him, but I don't know how to help him. He looks at me with these sad eyes, and I just don't know what I can do to make it all okay again." Aunt Penny flipped the last sandwich onto the plate, turned off the burner, and giggled nervously. "Isn't it silly that I keep thinking about a Confederate soldier I never even knew? A guy who may have never existed." She rubbed her upper arms and smiled a little too big. "It must be this town," she said. "We're surrounded by Civil War stuff, so we can't help thinking about it!"

Chucky didn't hear the last few words she said. His heart was racing. He was putting it all together. The soldier that Aunt Penny was dreaming of was a Confederate. How had he forgotten that? And the soldier in the cellar was a Confederate. *Was she dreaming about the ghost who shared her home? Or was it real? Was he coming to her at night while they slept? Was he coming to her for help?*

* * * * *

"I've been thinking about it and thinking about it, and I think I have an idea," Chucky said.

"You *think* you have an idea? You don't *know* if you have an idea?" Zach teased.

"Zach, don't be funny! I'm serious."

"I'm listening," Corporal Scott said. He had walked beside Philip, just behind Chucky and Zach as they hiked up the wooded trail. They'd told Aunt Penny they wanted to explore the patch of woods beyond the stone fence when they really wanted to catch up with Jared and find out what they should do next. But the corporal didn't have any ideas. Now Jared sat down on a big log on the side of the trail. Zach plopped down beside him.

Chucky faced the ghost soldier. "You have friends who served with the South?"

"Yes. I do. Why do you ask?"

"Wouldn't he talk to one of them? I mean, I was thinking about the Confederate soldier at Ghost Ring Hill. He was nice. Maybe he could..."

"He saluted you, Chucky!" Zach burst with excitement. "He said he would be proud to..."

Jared smiled at Zach's enthusiastic outburst. "He did salute you," he remembered. "I guess I could call him. He's a generous sort of fellow."

Philip had been silent on the walk. Now he looked hopeful. "Will you talk to him?" he asked the corporal.

"I'll meet him tonight and we'll talk." Jared rubbed his jaw thoughtfully. "It is hard," he said, "seeing boys still hurting from the war. Back then we all hurt every day. There were blistered feet and boots that fell apart while we marched. There was hunger so bad that it made hardtack taste good. There was the pain of watching your friends die, and of knowing the next guy you face in war might be an old friend, or family from back home." He rubbed his jaw again. "But it's supposed to be all over now. It's supposed to be done with."

Chucky blinked hard.

Zach watched the corporal's face as sadness enveloped him.

"But we *can* help the ghost in Aunt Penny's root cellar," Philip said resolutely. "I know we can."

Jared stood, brushing off the seat of his pants. "Yes, I think we can, too," he agreed.

They walked awhile quietly. They came to a section of pine trees with a small clearing. Their footsteps no longer crunched, cushioned by thick brown pine needles. The air was pungent with the sweet aroma of pine. As they rounded the bend, a half-grown fawn leaped to its feet and stared at them with wide eyes, knees locked in a V-shape. For a half second Chucky met its gaze, then the fawn leaped through the thick brush. There was a flash of its white tail and a spotted back, and then, it was gone. Chucky exhaled. "Wow. He was pretty."

Jared cleared his throat. "He was a cute whippersnapper," he said with a smile.

"Jared, I've been wondering." Philip had already forgotten the deer. "How are you going to find your, um, friend."

"I'll meet him on the hill, the one you call Ghost Ring Hill. We meet there often."

Zach had zeroed in on Philip's train of thought and now he took over. "But how will you get home? We can't ask Aunt Penny to take us back to the campground where we just visited. She'd want to know why."

Jared laughed. "Why, I'll walk," he said. "I believe I can remember the way."

"But that's a good 6 miles across town!" Zach was wide-eyed.

Jared looked amused. "Six miles? That's all?" He ruffled Zach's hair. "We traveled twenty, thirty miles a day during the war. Six miles is nothing!"

“Oh.” Philip stepped over another log, and continued to follow the wooded trail.

“When will you go?” Chucky wanted to know.

“I’ll go this evening. If all goes well I will be back in a day or so.”

“Is there anything we should do until you get back?”

“No, Chucky. Just help Aunt Penny. Talk to her. She needs you too.”

Jared’s words hung in the air. The three boys were wondering the same thing. *Should we tell Aunt Penny about the ghost?*

Chapter Eight

The Ghost in Chucky's Dream

"Why can't we do like we did before?" Zach asked as they walked back towards the house. "When Mr. Creach was having trouble with the RV we told him we had a friend that knew about ghosts and stuff."

Philip tossed a pebble into the field. "That won't work. For one thing, Aunt Penny would expect to see this friend of ours in the flesh and we can't tell her about Jared. Plus, I think it might be best if we manage to take care of it without telling her anything at all. As long as Jared can get back here with help, we should be okay."

"Yeah," Chucky said. "But we only *have* a few days left here. I'd feel just awful if we had to leave and both your aunt and the ghost still had their problems." Chucky took his Pirates cap from his head and slapped his thigh. "Why can't ghosts and people just be friends? It would be so much simpler!"

Philip grinned. He took Chucky's cap and put it back on his head. "Don't get agitated," he said. "It's just the way it is. We'll be helpful to Aunt Penny like Jared asked us to. That's all we can do right now."

Back at the house they were surprised to see Aunt Penny at the kitchen table with a stranger. "Oh, hello," Philip said.

"Boys, this is Mrs. Haws and she lives in the yellow house down the road. She came to introduce herself."

"You didn't say you had boys!" the lady said, standing up to greet the boys.

"Oh, they're my helpers, my nephews, Philip, and Zach, and their friend Chucky."

The boys shook hands with Mrs. Haws, whose face grew wide when she smiled. Her dark hair was peppered with gray, and she was so tall that Philip figured she was taller than Jared. She pointed to the table. "Have some apple cake."

Aunt Penny got extra glasses from the cabinet and poured lemonade into them. Chucky pulled the stool from the corner of the kitchen so they could all fit at the table. The apple cake was good, and the boys dove into it while the ladies talked.

"My husband will keep your mower in good repair."

"That's good to know. How long have you been living here, Mrs. Haws?"

"Twenty years in this place, but I've always lived in the area."

Aunt Penny took a sip of her lemonade. "Did you know the people who lived here last? I heard they have been gone for quite a while."

"Yes, this place sat empty for a few years. We worried it would just crumble. A house needs a person, you know. The very last people who lived here were a young couple. They only stayed a year. The owners before that were here before I came." She looked at the boys with wide eyes and lowered her voice, leaning over the table like she had a secret to tell. "Do you want to know what the young couple said?"

"Yes!" Zach answered, his imagination caught by the visitor's manner.

"Well, it's silly really, but that young couple said they never got a night's rest. The wife said that she had bad dreams and her husband couldn't do anything to calm her down."

Aunt Penny's fork clattered to her cake plate. "Bad dreams?"

The boys went still, shooting wild glances at each other and then looking at Aunt Penny who was growing pale.

"Dreams, yes. Now, wouldn't sleeping pills be better than giving up a house? I would think so. But they swore it was due to a ghost. The couple moved and the bank took over the property. Of course, the bank couldn't sell it right away, and I guess everyone is glad that a nice person like you bought it. We'd have hated to see it torn down. It's such a nice old house."

Aunt Penny nodded and absently went back to eating her cake.

"Ghosts aren't all bad," Chucky blurted. "And they will go away if their problems are solved. Ouch!"

Philip had kicked his shin! "Chucky reads a lot," he said in explanation.

Mrs. Haws laughed. "That's good," she said. "My kids were all readers, and they are all smart."

The conversation turned to the Haws' children and things settled down to normal. Aunt Penny lost some of her sickly look, and the boys got back to their cake and their own thoughts. By the time Mrs. Haws left, with a promise of a few divided houseplants, Aunt Penny seemed fine.

Philip took the plates to the sink. "Do you want me to wash these, or should I wait for supper dishes?"

Aunt Penny leaned against the counter. "I'll do supper dishes if you clean these for me. I'm having spaghetti tonight. Do you boys like spaghetti?"

"Yes," they answered.

"Good. Then, wash and dry these dishes, and why don't you lounge the rest of the day? You've been working very hard, and we're nearly finished. I think I'm going to go up and read for a while. You don't mind, do you?"

"We don't mind, Aunt Penny." Philip wanted to ask if she was upset about the things Mrs. Haws had said, but he thought it might be better to say nothing. He didn't want to upset her.

It didn't take long for the boys to do the dishes. They stood quietly together, with only the sound of sloshing, wiping, and clinking interrupting their thoughts. After Zach put the last fork in the drawer, they headed out the back door.

The day had become very warm. They headed to some shade near the edge of the yard and plopped down onto the grass.

"I wish we could tell her it will be okay," Philip said, his eyes on the cellar door.

Zach blew a puff of air up to lift his bangs. "But like you said, we'd have to explain everything to her. And I guess we can't. You're right. She'd tell Dad for sure."

Chucky took his ball cap off and lay back, his hands under his head. "And if your dad knew about Corporal Scott, who knows what he'd think."

Philip joined Chucky on his back. "We have to wait for Jared," he said. "That's all there is to it."

* * * * *

That night Aunt Penny left the kitchen door open and locked the screen door. She put a fan there so it would blow cool air into the living room and onto the air mattress where the boys slept. "This should be nice and cool for you, but if you get too warm, move the mattress into the kitchen."

"Thanks, Aunt Penny," Philip said. "Good night."

They watched her go up the stairs, and saw the light click off when she reached the top. Philip laid his head down on the cool pillowcase and hoped she'd get a good night's sleep. He was about to say this out loud when a large croaking sound next to him made him jump.

"Chucky!" Zach hissed.

"Sorry, it was a garlic bread burp," Chucky said.

They laughed and then grew quiet. All three were tired, and even with all the worries in his head, Chucky couldn't keep his eyes open. The cool air floated over his cheek and he drowsed.

* * * * *

"Why don't you read it?" the soldier said. He was very frustrated, Chucky could tell. He looked at Chucky with so many lines over his eyes that his forehead looked like a plowed field.

"I don't know what you mean," Chucky said. "Read what?"

"The letter I left. It's right here and I've been asking someone to read it."

Chucky saw that the man's trousers were torn, the left knee completely gone, and scratches covered the dirty kneecap. He was crouching, the bare knee poking through the hole in the trousers. Where were they? Chucky looked around. It was dark.

"You brought the enemy right to me, and didn't even hear my side," the soldier said.

"I don't know what you mean." Chucky felt like running, but couldn't move. "I'm scared," Chucky told him.

The soldier stood. "I'm scared too! And you nearly got me captured before I could tell my side."

"No, no." Chucky tried to look around. Then suddenly, he knew where he was! In the cellar! "Why are we here?"

"My letter!" The soldier pointed at his feet, leaned in the corner. "My letter will tell you my story." He

thrust his hand out and pointed to the ground at his feet.

"Okay. I'll try to help you, really."

* * * * *

Chucky sat up, sweat covering his forehead. It was still dark, still night, and he was still on the air mattress between Philip and Zach. It had been a dream. With careful movements Chucky rose and went into the kitchen. His legs tingled from the air coming from the fan near the door. He walked around it and pressed his nose to the screen.

We have to go into the cellar and find that letter, he thought.

Chucky took a deep breath. It didn't seem strange to him that he had been given a message by dreaming. It didn't seem strange to him that he was convinced he'd been talking to a ghost. So much had happened since they'd found Corporal Scott that he thought it even stranger that most people didn't know at least one ghost.

A prickle ran across his neck and he saw a misty shape by the back wall. He knew it was the soldier, and he knew the soldier could see him. With a calm mind and heart Chucky lifted his hand in a wave. The mist faded and was gone.

Chapter Nine

Digging Up the Clue

Chucky stared out of the screen door at the spot where the soldier had stood only seconds ago. His heart was racing, but strangely enough, it wasn't fear, but excitement. He found it hard to tear his eyes away from the spot where the ghost had been, but finally he did, because he needed to know if Philip or Zach had heard or seen anything.

In the living room, the bump of Zach's body groaned and moved slightly away from where Chucky sat. It was obvious he was deep in dreamland.

Philip lay on his back, very still. Without his glasses, he looked more like Zach than Chucky had ever noticed before. But unlike Zach, he was motionless, in deep sleep.

"Guys," Chucky said, his voice quivering. "Get up!"

Philip stirred, opened his eyes, and looked at Chucky. He reached for his glasses as he sat up. "What's up, Chucky?"

"The ghost. It was here."

"Here? In this room?" Philip's blue eyes were wide behind his glasses. His hair stood up in spikes from sleeping on it. He looked a little scared.

Chucky pointed through the opening, out to where the soldier had stood. "He talked to me."

"He what?" Philip was wide awake now, fear written across his face.

"Well, he sort of talked to me."

Philip's voice rose, and with it Zach sat up. "He did or he didn't. Which is it?"

"Who? Did or didn't what?" Zach was confused, and a little irritated at being awakened. "What are you two talking about? Do you know what time it is?"

Philip turned on Zach. "Oh, hush. We don't care about your beauty rest. Chucky said the ghost was here!"

Zach fell quiet, unable to speak as he looked around the dimly lit room. Only a patch of light fell across the floor, seeping through the window from the porch light. Then he whispered, "What was he doing?"

"Chucky said he talked to him. Sort of. Well, Chucky, did he speak to you or not?"

"You don't have to get mean about it," Chucky retorted, his face reflecting hurt. "I think he talked to me while I slept. He came to me in a dream." His face lit up. "Like he does to Aunt Penny! And when I awoke and was thinking that dream was pretty real, I got up and looked outside, and then I saw him standing there, just watching me." He shivered.

Philip was stunned. Chucky had never stood his ground like that before. "I'm sorry," he said slowly. "I was just scared."

"*Was* scared? I still am!" Zach gulped and pulled the blanket up to his chin. "It's not still here, is it?"

Chucky shook his head sadly.

"What did he say?" Philip questioned.

"He wanted to know why we haven't read his letter."

"What letter?" Philip's brow was furrowed.

Chucky shrugged and went on. "He said it's right here and he's been asking someone to read it."

Zach gasped. "Aunt Penny! He's been asking Aunt Penny to read it. He talked to her in her dreams too!"

Philip shuddered. "The penny that kept coming back? Do you think he was trying to tell us to get Aunt Penny to help?"

All three boys stared at each other, the light on the floor flickering between them as the curtains blew out. A rumble of thunder broke the silence. A storm was brewing outside.

Chucky nodded. "It makes sense," he said.

"What else did he say?" Zach eagerly wanted to know.

"He said he was scared. Imagine that? *He* was scared. He wanted to know why we brought the enemy to him."

"Jared." Zach and Philip spoke at the same time.

Remembering the ghost's haunted face, Chucky wanted to cry. "He was so desperate. He wants us to find his letter."

"Did he tell you where it is?" Philip pressed.

"No, but in my dream he was in the root cellar, and he was pointing to the ground, over in the corner. I think it's buried."

"We'll have to dig."

Zach rolled his eyes at Philip. "Of course we'll have to dig. But should we tell Aunt Penny? I mean, it seems he was trying to tell her all along."

Chucky and Philip were thinking. Philip finally shook his head. "I don't think we should. At least, not yet. He was probably trying to tell Aunt Penny because she is an adult. He probably thinks we are just kids."

"But he came to me!" Chucky protested.

Philip touched Chucky's arm. "He came to you after we took Jared to him. Now we have to try to help. We have to dig."

* * * * *

It had taken forever to get back to sleep. Part of Chucky believed he never did sleep, so restless was his night. The next day had gone slowly, with Aunt Penny getting them to help her rearrange furniture and to dust each room. She even sent them out to pick vases of wildflowers. "This place is starting to look and feel like a home," she said. Once or twice Philip caught her looking at them oddly, as though she knew something was wrong, but didn't want to pry.

At lunch, Aunt Penny set her glass of iced tea down firmly on the table, and said, "You boys have been working way too much. What do you want to do this afternoon?"

Dig in the root cellar, Zach thought.

"Go exploring again," Philip said.

"Then, get outta here," Aunt Penny said, smiling broadly. "You guys need to have some fun. The park land is just over the stone wall and across that field, where there is so much more history for you to uncover."

Boy, is she right, Zach thought, his mind on the letter he wanted to uncover.

And so they set out, across the stone wall, through the stubbly farm field and into the cool forest of the parkland. Shortly, they returned and listened for Aunt Penny humming in the back room. At last they stole across the yard.

Chucky lifted the heavy root cellar door and they crept down the steps.

After Philip had pulled the light cord, Chucky lowered and closed the door behind them.

Aunt Penny must have changed the light bulb, Chucky thought. The dark, musty smell of the cellar filled his nostrils, and he breathed deeper. It was a comforting smell, somehow.

"Where did he want us to dig?" Philip asked.

Chucky looked around the dark root cellar, trying to picture where the soldier had crouched. "I think it was there," he said, pointing to a corner near two wooden shelves of canning jars, "but I'm not sure."

"It's a place to start," Zach said. He pointed at the assortment of tools leaning in the corner. An old mattock, a shovel with a big chip out of the blade, and a pitchfork.

Philip picked up the shovel and carried it to the corner. He tried to push it into the packed earthen floor, but the shovel didn't even make a dent. Next, he stood it upright and jumped on the top of the blade. Still, it didn't slide into the earth. Instead, Philip tumbled off sideways.

"What the heck," Philip grumbled. "If this old shovel won't cut through it, what will?"

Zach had the pitchfork in his hands. "Let me try to loosen up the dirt with this." Similarly, Zach jumped on the shoulders of the fork tines, piercing the earth an inch or so.

Chucky groaned. "This is going to take forever."

Philip nodded, and Zach positioned himself to use the pitchfork again. "At least we have all afternoon," he huffed.

It took almost an hour to loosen up the patch of earth. Chucky and Philip pitched in while Zach rested. Philip found an old hand trowel, and Chucky pulled a big tablespoon from his jangling pockets. Together, they scooped out loose dirt, little by little.

Clang!

The boys jumped when Chucky's spoon hit something hard and hollow sounding.

"Oh boy," Zach mumbled. He was on his knees, stretching tall, looking over them at the widening hole.

The boys took turns digging until they saw a glitter of glass, the top of a Mason jar.

"Another jar?" Chucky sounded disappointed.

Philip cleared dirt from the top of it, peering inside. "But this one has something inside," he said.

Both boys stopped digging. Looking into the hole, the boys noticed the top of the jar was milky with age. Through the wavy old glass, they could see the soft folds of paper.

"The letter," Chucky said, his heart beating a tattoo in his chest.

Chapter Ten

The War Is Over

"Oh my gosh," Zach whispered. "It's all real."

"Of course it's real," Philip said as he wiped his forehead. "Chucky, hold on to that jar; Zach and I will pat this dirt down in place again so Aunt Penny won't see it."

Chucky cradled the jar in the crook of his arm and studied the rusted metal lid that had last been touched over 140 years ago. With a fingernail he picked at the edge of it and it flaked apart. "I wonder if we'll be able to touch the letter," he said aloud.

Zach grunted as he helped his brother pack the dirt into the hole. "Let's hope Jared comes and all of this can be solved."

Chucky could hear Aunt Penny walking in the kitchen above him. A thought came to him, bringing a sense of calm with it. It settled over his body like a blanket. "You're right, Zach. It will be all right, for everyone."

"Let's take the letter out on the other side of the stone wall to read it," Philip said, putting the shovel back in the corner. He put his finger to his lips. "Don't let her hear us leaving."

As warm as they had been while digging in the cellar, the fresh air outside was even warmer, but there was a breeze and it prickled the back of Chucky's neck. He hugged the jar to himself and crept behind the other two. They scrambled over the wall and hunkered behind it.

Chucky held the jar and wiped it with his hands. It was narrower at the top than at the bottom, and he scraped the dirt off it until he could read the impressed letters on its side: Mason's Patent, Nov 30th, 1858. "Whoa," he whispered. "It's so old."

"Give me that jar, and the spoon from your pocket," Philip asked him. Chucky handed both of them to him and watched as Philip chipped away at the lid with the spoon.

"Be careful," Zach said.

"I am."

It took only a moment for the main part of the lid to chip and fall away. Philip looked at the other two and then shook the jar upside down to shake the rolled paper toward its mouth. With agonizing slowness he reached into the jar with two fingers to grasp the paper. "Got it," he said and pulled it out.

"It's in pretty good shape," Chucky said.

"It's not crumbly anyway," Philip said. He began to open the roll to lay it flat. It was amazing to see the stark dark letters on the old yellowish paper. The words had been written in pencil with a heavy hand.

I don't know why I ran like rabit from the yanks. I am afrade I cannot go back and if I stay in this hole I will be found. My belly is crampt and my feet is bleeding, If I staid with the company I cood be in the fiting now. Cant make it back now. I am sorry. Did not mean to drop my gun and run. I will be lost and labeled diserter and I am not one. Tell my famly. David Har

"That's it? He didn't even finish writing his name. Corporal Scott said it was Harmon," Chucky said. "What could have happened?"

Philip let the paper curl into its age-old roll and slipped it back into the jar. "And if he didn't finish writing his name, he sure didn't bury the letter himself."

Zach whistled. "You're right, Philip. Someone must have caught him, and someone else must have buried the letter."

"But why bury the letter?" Chucky asked. "And why is he haunting the cellar if he made it out of here as a prisoner, or whatever?"

Philip looked across the field to the woods and wondered the same things. He also figured it would be dark in another five hours, and maybe the darkness would bring Jared Scott and the answers they wanted.

* * * * *

"Son, wake up," the voice said.

Philip looked up at the man calling him, blinked once, then sat bolt upright. "Jared," he whispered. "I didn't mean to fall asleep." He jostled Chucky and Zach. "Wake up."

Chucky was glad to see Jared, and surprised when they followed him through the kitchen to discover that it was midnight. They tiptoed to the screen door and opened it quietly. The moon shone in a clear sky. Chucky bumped into Philip, who stopped short of the doorsill, and he looked up to find the reason looking back at him.

The Confederate officer he'd talked to on Ghost Ring Hill, the night they scared the ghost hunter, was standing in the yard. His golden braid shimmered and the plume in his hat brim waved in the breeze.

"Hello, sir," Chucky said to him, venturing closer. "I just know you can help David."

"David? You know his name?" Jared asked.

Philip explained the letter they'd found in the root cellar. "I put it back on the steps, inside the cellar door."

Jared turned to the officer. "Colonel? This way."

Three boys and a Confederate colonel followed Jared to the cellar doors. "His name must be David Harmon, Colonel. I sensed the name Harmon the first time I tried to help him, but he didn't trust a Yankee and I couldn't find out any more. Since we now know the problem, perhaps you can set things straight with him."

"Yes, I'll try." The colonel turned to Chucky. "I'm glad to see you again, all of you. Follow at will." He touched the brim of his hat and walked down into the cellar, right through the door!

"That just kills me," Zach said with a shiver.

Jared chuckled. "Perhaps I should stay outside."

The boys lifted the cellar door and laid it back. The officer gave off a glow similar to Jared's and they could see well enough to make it down the steps into the cool, damp cellar. Chucky moved closest to the officer and stared into the corner.

"These boys have found you, and they've asked me to come. I know you are ready to leave here, aren't you? You mustn't feel bound here. You don't need to be here any longer. David Harmon, isn't it?"

The boys could see a foggy blur in the corner. It seemed to grow taller, as if a person was crouching in the corner and decided to stand upright. Slowly, an image appeared of a young man, in ragged clothes and bare feet. His sad face was focused on the colonel and he made an effort to salute. Without warning, his shoulders slumped and he covered his face with his hands.

Philip heard a low rumble.

"But there's no need to feel ashamed," the colonel said. "I find no fault in you, son."

The rumble became choppy, and Philip realized the sound was words. He could hear the ghost speaking, the words becoming clearer.

"...thought I was dying. The man came in...There was a gun...shot me. The lady cried. I gave...letter. She was sorry, said she'd see it safe."

The colonel motioned with his hand to stop him. "I'm sure the man thought he was doing right. Men at war always think they are doing right. But that war is over. More have come and gone as well. There may always be war, but you have done your share and your war is over. Come out of this cellar, and out of this house. You can go home, or you can go elsewhere, but first, please come with me." He extended his arm to the soldier.

The soldier stepped from the corner, then stopped. He looked at the boys who stood there stationary as posts. “Who are they, sir?”

The colonel smiled at the boys. “They are friends of ours who happen to be able to see us. We are what the living call ghosts, and not all of the living can see us. Isn’t that right, boys?”

Chucky, who was excited about the colonel coming to their aid, snapped to attention. “Yes, sir!” he yelped. Philip and Zach shushed him.

David Harmon looked at them, then at his hands. “So, I’m a ghost for sure.”

“You sure are,” Zach whispered confidently.

The boys cleared the way for the colonel and the soldier. As they passed by Chucky, the soldier looked at him and smiled. “I talked to you. And to the lady who lives here. Didn’t I?”

Chucky nodded. “You came to us in our dreams. We wanted to help you.”

“You’ve done it. Thank you.”

Outside the boys saw the soldier hesitate when he saw Jared Scott. But Jared smiled at him. “Hello, David. Like the colonel said, ‘Our war is over.’” He offered his hand and waited. David Harmon brushed his hand along his pant leg and put it into Jared’s.

"I guess that's about it, boys," Jared said. "I'll see you when you come home. You should see the way Casey trots that little white dog around, Chucky."

Chucky groaned. "Don't remind me of it. Why can't we have a dog like Boo?"

Jared laughed. "But you do have a dog like Boo. You have Boo. And he's just waiting for you to come home and scratch his ears. Bye, fellows."

"Good-bye," they said, and Chucky saluted the colonel.

The boys watched the three ghosts fade from sight. Philip sighed. "Well, here we are, barefoot, outside, and in the middle of the night."

"Let's shut the cellar door and get inside," Zach said.

Chucky raced for the jar. "We should take this in with us," he said. "Maybe if we tell your aunt about finding the letter she'll feel better. She'll have a reason for why she dreamed and since he's gone the dreams will be gone. She'll just think it was one of those weird things that happen sometimes."

Philip quietly closed the cellar door. "You know, weird things happen to us all the time since Jared came into our lives."

Zach laughed. "Actually, Philip, if you think seriously about it we never had anything weird happen to us until Chucky's mom moved to the campground. I think it's Chucky."

"Oh yeah, sure," Chucky said, but laughed with them. Zach and Philip were his best friends. "If I hadn't come along, you would be two bored guys."

All was quiet in the house. Chucky put the jar with its letter on a living room windowsill. While Philip and Zach straightened the blanket on the air mattress he went to the end table where he'd dumped the stuff from his pants' pockets earlier. Smiling, he plucked the penny from the pile and let it drop into the jar with the letter.

"The start of the mystery and the end of it, right in the jar," Chucky said.

"That's neat," Philip whispered. "Now come on and get back into bed. We have to figure out what we are going to do now."

Chucky plopped down between them, making the mattress bounce a little. "I think you should tell your aunt everything."

"Not everything," Zach said. "Do you really want to tell her about Jared? She still might tell Dad."

"Okay," Philip said. "We'll go halfway. I say we tell her we knew there was a ghost. But what else do we say?"

"Tell her the truth about my dream," Chucky said. "She dreamed, too. But my dream told me more and we found the letter. We can say we saw him leave."

"And that is totally true," Zach said. "We did see him leave."

Philip nodded. "I think that she'll promise not to tell Dad if we ask her not to. Don't you? After all, she won't want him worrying about her either."

"It's worth a try," Chucky said. "Do we all agree?" Chucky put one hand out, palm up. First, Zach, then Philip put their hands down upon it. "Okay then!"

"Right," said Philip. "Now, let's get some sleep. Sweet dreams, you two."

The boys laughed, snuggling into their pillows. Chucky looked forward to morning when they could put Aunt Penny's mind at ease about her mysterious dreams. He grinned in the dark and inched away from the elbow near his ribs. It wasn't so bad being in the middle.

Fact-finders

Look for books about ghosts or the Civil War in your school and public libraries. For more information on the Battle of Gettysburg and the supposed ghosts that haunt that area, here are two places for you to contact.

Gettysburg National Military Park
1195 Baltimore Pike
Gettysburg, Pennsylvania 17325
(717) 334-1124

Or visit the National Park Service on the web at www.nps.gov and follow the links to the park of your choice.

Ghosts of Gettysburg
271 Baltimore Street
Gettysburg, Pennsylvania 17325
(717) 337-0445
www.ghostsofgettysburg.com

Call or write to find out how to order Mark Nesbitt's books or take a ghost tour of Gettysburg. Tell Mr. Nesbitt the Gettysburg Ghost Gang sent you!

If you'd like to see a Gettysburg Ghost Gang Club formed, send a postcard with your name and address to:

Gettysburg Ghost Gang
P.O. Box 70
Arendtsville, Pennsylvania 17303

The Authors

SHELLEY SYKES has always been interested in ghosts and history. Living near the Gettysburg National Military Park gives her the opportunity to learn more about both. Her first young adult novel, *For Mike*, received an Edgar Allan Poe Award nomination for best young adult mystery and has been nominated for several state book awards. When not writing, Shelley Sykes is active in Girl Scouts and investigates ghosts and haunted locations.

LOIS SZYMANSKI is the author of 15 books for young readers, including *Little Icicle* and *Sea Feather*. She is the only author in the state of Maryland to start a writing club for children, under the umbrella of the 4-H program. She also created a program in which children can exhibit their writing at a county fair, and have it evaluated by professional writers from the community. Lois Szymanski has written for numerous children's publications, including *Highlights For Children* and *U*S*Kids Magazine*. She is regional advisor for the Maryland/Delaware/West Virginia sector of the Society of Children's Book Writers and Illustrators.

THE GHOST COMES OUT: *Gettysburg Ghost Gang #1*

The discovery of a ghost at the Gettysburg Battlefield is just the beginning of many adventures for three young friends.

978-1-57249-266-0 • PB

GHOST ON BOARD: *Gettysburg Ghost Gang #2*

Three young friends must rely on the help of their ghost-friend, Corporal Jared Scott, to solve the mystery of a new ghost that appears at the Cavalry Ridge Campground.

978-1-57249-267-7 • PB

NIGHTMARE: *Gettysburg Ghost Gang #3*

An eerie encounter with what turns out to be a ghost-horse sends the boys scrambling to their ghost-friend, Corporal Jared Scott, for help.

978-1-57249-268-4 • PB

GHOST HUNTER: *Gettysburg Ghost Gang #4*

Philip, Zach, and Chucky find themselves in a ghostly jam at Cavalry Ridge Campground when a ghost hunter arrives in Gettysburg.

978-1-57249-298-1 • PB

WHITE MANE PUBLISHING CO., INC.

To Request a Catalog Please Write to:

WHITE MANE PUBLISHING COMPANY, INC.
P.O. Box 708 • Shippensburg, PA 17257
e-mail: marketing@whitemane.com
Our catalog is also available online
www.whitemane.com

CPSIA information can be obtained
at www.ICGtesting.com
Printed in the USA
BVOW06s0309160517
483581BV00008B/7/P